NOBODY HAS TIME FOR ME

NOBODY HAS TIME FOR ME

A Modern Fairy Tale told by Vladimír Škutina

and illustrated by Marie-José Sacré

WELLINGTON PUBLISHING

Chicago

Nobody Has Time for Me

From the Czech original *Kde bydlí čas*
translated by Dagmar Herrmann

Copyright © 1988 by Bohem Press, Zurich and Prague
English translation copyright © 1991 by Dagmar Herrmann

Published in the United States of America in 1991

Wellington Publishing, Inc.
P.O. Box 14877
Chicago, Illinois 60614

Library of Congress Cataloging-in-Publication Data

Škutina, Vladimír
[Kde bydlí čas. English]
Nobody has time for me: a modern fairy tale/told by Vladimír Škutina and
illustrated by Marie-José Sacré.
    p.   cm.
Translation of: Kde bydlí čas.
Summary: Karin's meeting with Father Time teaches her that people can
find time for each other if they make proper use of their time.
[1. Time—Fiction.] I. Sacré, Marie-José, ill. II. Title.
PZ7.S62875No 1991   91-4457
[E]—dc20

ISBN 0-922984-07-7

Binding reinforced for library use
Printed and bound in Italy

It was snowing. Karin stood by the window, looking out into the dusk. No one had time for her.

"Tell me about Time. Please, Daddy."
"I don't have time, can't you see?" grumbled Karin's father, his eyes glued to the television set. He was watching the football game and reading the paper at the same time.
"Will *you* tell me a story about Time?" Karin asked her brother. "Leave me alone," he snapped, running past her, "I don't have time for dumb questions."
Karin quietly slipped into the kitchen.
Her mother was ironing and baking cookies.
The sweet smell of the holidays filled the house.
"Mommy, how does Time look?"
"You can't draw a picture of it," replied Karin's mother. She was checking the oven to see that the cookies didn't burn. "Time is an awful thing," she muttered. Karin left the kitchen, walked through the living room and into the hall. No one paid attention to her. She put on her coat and stepped into the street. The face on the clock tower shone brightly.

"That's where Time must live," Karin whispered.

In the courtyard in front of the clock tower the iron gate stood wide open. In the dust of the fresh snow there were footprints. Huge footprints. They were leading to the tower. "An awful Thing," Karin thought to herself. Her mother's words sounded in Karin's head.

"Time is an awful Thing," her mother had said. "At the end of the day, Time takes back everything it gives people in the morning."

Karin pushed hard on the heavy wooden door. The door
flew open. She looked around and carefully tiptoed in.
Before her rose an old winding stone stairway. The wind
slammed the door behind her. Startled, she pressed herself
against the wall. A chip of plaster dropped at her feet.

"An awful Thing," her mother's words echoed in
Karin's ears.

Karin was sure she had landed in a fairy tale. She would
not be frightened. In fairy tales, nothing bad ever happened
to children if they were brave.
"You awful Thing, you!" Karin yelled up the tower, "I'm
not scared of you!" The echo returned her shout. Nothing
happened. Slowly, Karin began climbing the first step.
Something rubbed against her face. She jumped aside.
When her eyes got used to the dark, Karin saw that it was
just a rope, dangling in the air. She straightened up
and moved on.
"Mr. Time!" Karin called into the tower. "Don't be scared!
It's only me, Karin! I won't hurt you! I just want to see
where you live! If you aren't home, I'll come back!"
She kept climbing.

At the head of the stairs was an open, square space
surrounded by high walls. Soft light coming from the clock
faces filled the room. An enormous clockwork with cog
wheels, chains and ropes loomed above her. A pendulum
steadily counted the seconds. The wind whistled between
the ticks of the clock. Suddenly, the machinery began
rumbling, the chains started to rattle and the cog wheels
creaked. The clock struck the half hour. The tower shook.

High on a wooden balcony, an old man had stepped from the shadows. His smile was all mischief.

"Time," breathed Karin, "Father Time."

"You aren't nice to people," Karin blurted out as the old man came down the steps. "You don't give grown-ups time to play with their children. Nobody has time for me. Not my father, not my mother, not even my brother. No one. I am sad. I am lonely."

The closer Father Time came, the better Karin felt, for he looked something like her grandfather. "I found you, at last," Karin said with relief. "I've been looking for you, only I couldn't figure out where you live."

"Then one day, my brother told me that Time lived in a clock. So, first I took apart Daddy's wristwatch, but Time didn't live there. How could it? A watch is too small. Then I pulled up a chair to our cuckoo clock, but when I peeked in, it crashed to the floor. That really did it! Daddy said it was high Time something be done with me. That's when I knew that Time must live up high. In the tower! Now tell me, what do you do all day long?"

"All day long, time keeps running," answered the old man with a smile. "The clock wheels spin and turn and people spin and turn."

"Then do me a favor. Stop running just for a while," Karin said. "I'll rush home, and Mom, Dad, and my brother will all have time for me."
"I'm sorry, I can't do that. Time can't be stopped, my dear," said the little old man.
"But in fairy tales everything is possible!" Karin exclaimed.
"Would you want fairy tales to become real?" asked the old man.
Karin's eyes beamed. "I sure would," she said with excitement.
"Then devils and dragons, witches and sorcerers would also become real," said the man.
That scared her. "Awful Things too?"
"Yes, awful things too," he answered.
"Mom said Time was an awful Thing."

The old man smiled again. "Sometimes yes, sometimes no. People who can't manage time run around like they're being chased. But those who know how to make time..."
"Did you say people could make Time?" Karin was beginning to think he was teasing her.
"Of course. Let me show you," the old man said.

He lifted Karin onto the sill beneath the clock tower window. "Look! People did all this. They built houses, paved streets, put together the whole town, with lights, cars, buses, everything. For all that, they needed time. And they had to make it.

"Time helps people, you see,
even though it's not around
as much as everyone would like."

"Help me down, please," Karin said. The view from the window had made her think of home. "How late is it?" She was worried.

"Soon my clock will strike six," said the old man. "Oh no," Karin fretted, "I'm supposed to be home by six." She headed for the steps, then stopped in her tracks. "I've got an idea! Could you stop yourself for a little while? Just this once?"

"Well…You know what? For you, I'll do it," said the old man, smiling exactly like Karin's grandfather smiled. "I'll make an exception. And do you know why?" Karin didn't.

"Because I am not Father Time. I am a clockmaker. I take care of this clock and fix it. If I were Time itself, I could never stop. But since I am only a time*keeper,* I will stop time for you." He climbed the ladder up to the clock face and stopped the enormous pendulum. All was quiet. Karin still thought she was being teased just a little, but she was glad that time had stopped, anyway. She said a hasty goodbye and scurried home.

When she ran in, Karin's father looked sternly at his wristwatch. In the kitchen, steam was rising from the soup. "You are late for dinner," he said with a frown. "You are supposed to be home by six. Where have you been?"

"In a fairy tale," said Karin, and stepped to the window. "Look, it's only six o'clock now." She pointed to the tower. Over the bustling city, the clock tower stood tall and bright. It showed six o'clock, exactly. The bells began to chime.

Karin's father and mother looked at each other and smiled.

When Karin was almost ready for bed, her parents asked to hear the fairy tale.

"It's about Time," Karin said, "and I'll tell you…if you make a little time for me."

Vladimír Škutina is a well known Czech writer and playwright. Born in Prague in 1931, he studied TV journalism and psychology, and gained notoriety as a TV commentator during the Prague Spring of 1968. After the Soviet invasion of Czechoslovakia, Škutina was jailed for four years and later spent ten years in exile in Switzerland. In the wake of the political changes that had swept Eastern Europe at the end of 1989, Škutina returned to his native city, and in 1990 was elected to the Czech National Assembly. The inspiration for *Nobody Has Time For Me* came from his daughter, Lucie.

Marie-José Sacré was born in 1946 in Belgium, where she continues to live and work. She studied at the Academy of Fine Arts in Liège. Her work has been exhibited throughout Europe, in Japan, and in the United States. For her children's book illustrations, she received the Youth Book Prize in France (1980) and the OWL Prize in Japan (1982).